AF491109

It's an INN-SIDE JOB

Tales of an Innkeeper

PART 2

KATHY BRANNING

ISBN 979-8-88943-145-9 (paperback)
ISBN 979-8-88943-146-6 (digital)

Copyright © 2023 by Kathy Branning

All rights reserved. No part of this publication may be reproduced, distributed, or transmitted in any form or by any means, including photocopying, recording, or other electronic or mechanical methods without the prior written permission of the publisher. For permission requests, solicit the publisher via the address below.

Christian Faith Publishing
832 Park Avenue
Meadville, PA 16335
www.christianfaithpublishing.com

Printed in the United States of America

This book is dedicated to my husband, Alex, who is my biggest cheerleader. You believe in me so much than you make me second-guess myself when I have doubt in my abilities.

And to my beautiful daughter, Ali, your strong conviction for justice and your support of my work means the world. All my love, my sweets.

Welcome back to Still Waters Inn! The last time we were together, I was presented with a life-changing opportunity to expand my inn and open other inns around the country. Spoiler alert, I said yes! I'm getting ready for my newest inn opening in upstate New York. Here I go again, putting the cart before the horse. Let's go back a bit so I can share with you my adventure and the tales of an innkeeper.

* * * * *

The smell of orange and cinnamon embraced me the moment I walked in the house. Home. My castle. The place where I found peace and serenity. Over the years, I've painstakingly made this house into a retreat, a place of calm in the storm of chaos that ensues outside of that front door. As I look around the entryway with all the arches and fresh paint, I sigh. Opening a new chapter almost always means closing an old one. No matter how much joy, excitement, and anticipation one might have for the new chapter, the old still demands our grieving, 25 percent excited, 75 percent terrified.

The living room beckons like a siren song. Come, it says. As I sit on the sofa, Molly, my bichon frise hops up and curls right up on my lap like a good little emotional support dog. I look around the room. I thought I'd be here forever, I never thought I'd be jet-setting around the world to run multiple inns. I know it's not forever, and I am grateful for Alan, and I decided to keep the house, but even so, renting it out to others still has me all up in my feelings, not to mention all the tiny details to figure out. Also, going to New York, even if for just a short time, is pretty terrifying.

My good friend Lynn keeps reminding me of all my favorite rom-coms that are set in New York, and honestly, it's pretty soothing when I think about Meg Ryan and Tom Hanks standing in Central Park. He wipes her tear with a handkerchief as he says, "Don't cry, shopgirl." Or Billy Crystal and Meg Ryan gallivanting around New York City as they fall madly in love with each other. Thinking about these scenes, although fiction, bring a smile immediately to my face.

"Knock, knock," Roxy says as she walks in the front door.

"Wait, hold the door!" yells Simone as she barrels up the walkway, hands full of three Dutch Bros' cold brews.

"Hey, guys, come on in." I grab my cold brew from Simone and plop back down to my spot on the couch, and Molly reclaims her spot on my lap. "Thanks for meeting with me this morning, and thanks for the coffee, Simone."

"So I'll cut to the chase. As you both know, we are moving forward on opening a new inn. We've decided after much deliberation with Donald and his people, New York will be our first—well, second inn—well, you know what I mean…"

"Wow, New York! I've always wanted to live on the East Coast," Simone responds in a short burst as she swirls her cold brew.

"That's actually kind of perfect because I wanted to ask you both if you would be willing to run my inn in New York."

"You mean like move there?" Roxy asks hesitantly.

"Yes, I know it's a big ask. You both have been such a huge part of the Still Waters success, and you both are always saying how you wish you could do it full time. I've been praying about it, and with your kids all almost totally grown, it seems like an ideal time. Just do me a favor and pray about it."

"I don't know. New York? No beach, crowded…that kind of living just isn't for me," Roxy states, "but I promise I will pray about. I'm always up for a God adventure."

"Oh! I love that! A God adventure! That's exactly what this is. Sorry, Roxy, I'm stealing that," I exclaim.

"Yes, I love that too," Simone adds. "So, Kate, how are you feeling about all this?"

"I mean it's a big move!" I respond. "But I know this is the right decision. You know when you just know in your knower?"

Roxy and Simone break out into a fit of laughter.

"What?" I sputter. Then I start laughing along with them. We laugh so hard I, of course, let out a snort, Simone grabs her stomach, and Roxy falls to the floor in a fit of laughter.

After the laughter dies down, we all catch our breath.

"You, guys, really are the best medicine," I say with emotion.

Roxy and Simone are two of my bestest friends. (Do I sound like a kindergartener?) No, but seriously, the amount of sass and compassion in each of these women is enough to make my heart swell. Okay…enough with the mushy stuff. Obviously, Roxy and Simone are exceptional human beings, and that's why I couldn't wait to invite them on this journey with me.

Simone is tall and spunky, with long brown hair and brown eyes usually framed by whatever colorful and fun frames she decided to wear that day. Today she has on a casual teal T-shirt dress and her teal and lime semicolon earrings, so of course, she has on her lime-green glasses to match. Simone has an enormous capacity for loving people and teaches me a great deal about what it means to be a friend. Roxy is my wild card with her dark medium-length hair and her red tips; she colors the ends of her hair a different vivid color all the time. She's wearing a black top with her designer jeans, her long coffin-shaped acrylic nails majestically painted in pink and red with hearts for Valentine's Day. You can always count on her nails being on point. Roxy is my karaoke buddy, a diva who is not afraid to take the mic and has a beautiful voice too.

Roxy, Simone, and I worked out all the details that pertain to running the new inn, whose responsibilities would belong to who. Simone was insistent that she would provide activities for the guest kids, and Roxy wanted to coordinate the events. The duties were evenly distributed among the three of us, and I felt pretty good about each of them being able to make an informed decision from here on out. Roxy and Simone agreed to go talk to their husbands and pray about this huge choice in front of them. The idea of three best friends running an inn together sounded great, but three thousand miles away. This would be a big move. I knew it was a lot to ask, but she also knew there was no one else I'd rather do it with.

Nikki, Mitchell, and Doug have Still Waters Inn pretty much dialed in(n). (See what I did there?) Nikki has assured me the inn is in good hands while I go open our new location in New York. I am one blessed woman to have so many quality people in my life.

Nikki and I hired a young sous-chef to train with her to help with the food as Nikki takes over most of my role with events. Mitchell is being promoted to manager assisting customers with their needs and overseeing check-ins and many other details. Our groundskeeper Doug has been an absolute godsend. He not only keeps the grounds pristine, much to our guests' delight, but he can also fix pretty much anything at all, which has been a huge blessing. This means our next event; the marriage retreat that Alan and I are doing should be smooth sailing. Between getting ready for the retreat in a little over a week and planning our new inn, my head is swirling.

Let's see, I have a lot of feelings about relocating to New York to run our newest inn. It's a bit taxiing…come on! You had to expect a pun was coming. I think we have well established by now just how humorous I am. I mean, I must be to survive in this world, am I right?

The other day as I was having said feelings, I decided to open up my Bible for a little wisdom and encouragement. Boy, did I find a whopper! Check this out:

> Afflicted city, storm-battered, unpitied: I'm about to rebuild you with stones of turquoise, lay your foundations with sapphires, construct your towers with rubies, Your gates with jewels, and all your walls with precious stones. All your children will have God for their teacher—what a mentor for your children! You'll be built solid, grounded in righteousness, far from any trouble—nothing to fear! Far from terror—it won't even come close! If anyone attacks you, don't for a moment suppose I sent them, and if any should attack, nothing will come of it. I create the blacksmith who fires up his forge and makes weapons designed to kill. I also create the destroyer—but no weapon that can hurt you has ever been forged. Any accuser who takes you to court will be dismissed as a liar. This is what God's servants can expect. I'll see that everything works out for the best. God's decree. (Isaiah 54:11–17)

These words have comforted me and have been a life source for me to keep coming back to when I feel weak. In this season, even more so than my humor, I've had to lean into God's promises and His strength to help me through. I know in the grand scheme of things my dream is happening, and it's so good, and I am extremely grateful, but it doesn't negate all the hard things.

As I clean up after my meeting with Roxy and Simone, discarding our empty Dutch Bros cups, I submit my plans to God. I'm such a planner, and sometimes that drives me to grab hold of all the reigns and try to control every single detail of my life. Lately this feels like it's been more of a struggle. I even wrote in my journal last month that my new goal is to go with the flow more. Take more risk. I can't help but laugh now as I look at the adventure ahead of me. I sit down with my planner—ironic, isn't it? And I see that the rest of the day is Alan and I finalizing our retreat. I close my planner and head out to the foyer just in time to see Alan walk in through the front door.

"Hey, babe!" I welcome him with a kiss.

"Hey, boo, you ready to work on retreat stuff?" replies Alan. He then returns the kiss, making it a tad bit deeper.

"Yep! Let me grab my laptop and my bag, and we can head out. I'm thinking Thai for lunch. Sound good to you?"

"Perfect! Yummy food, a lovely lady, and an afternoon of planning. Couldn't think of anything better."

"Thai Hut, it is!" I respond as I try to ignore his flirty response, but really what's the use, I know my face has already blushed. Even now after so many years, he can make me blush. How is that?

I grab my laptop and my purse and grab Alan's hand as we head out for our planning lunch date.

2

"Welcome to your marriage retreat, hosted by Still Waters Inn and Alan and Kate Brown. Alan and Kate Brown have a heart for marriage and family ministry and are so excited to provide this special time for each one of you to pour into your marriages. We hope you enjoy a fun weekend together as we dig into scripture to show God's design for igniting our marriages and share from our own joy and struggles along with a few other guest couple speakers. We'll lead seasoned couples and newlyweds alike through a series of talks bookended by two relaxing evenings in our Victorian Inn, in both times alone with your spouse and time spent in our carefully curated list of optional group activities such as a picnic and wine under the stars, canoeing or kayaking on the lake, and to end our weekend of connection, a Valentine's dance. We pray your time here is healing, restorative, and rejuvenating. Whether you're needing to reconnect with your spouse or just have some time away together, we hope you'll leave with some valuable tools and lots of love."

It's Friday, and Mitchell, our manager, has just started checking our couples in for the marriage retreat. Each room has a welcome basket with a note, the weekend itinerary, a bottle of wine with two wine glasses, and personalized T-shirts for each of them. Cheesy, I know, but Alan lives for cheese, so we compromise. We have check-in until 6:00 p.m., and then we start with a romantic Italian-themed dinner. Nikki has prepared tantalizing Italian dishes such as chicken parmesan, lasagna, and of course, spaghetti and meatballs. Very "Bella Notte"/*Lady and the Tramp* vibes, excuse me, while I'm singing, "This is the night, it's a beautiful night and they call it Bella Notte..." Sorry, I get carried away when it comes to themes.

"Nikki, do you need any extra hands in here?" I ask as I enter the kitchen.

"No, thanks, Kate, too many cooks in the kitchen, you know what I mean?" Nikki grumbled.

I throw my hands up and back away slowly. Nikki might take some time adjusting to having help; she and I are alike in that way. We like it done our way. Well, let me see, the tables are set with the stereotypical red gingham tablecloths, taper candles in a jug, and a place card so each couple knows where to sit. Since we don't normally serve dinner and our inn is fully booked with retreat guest, then we will be safe from anybody trying to come sit down for a meal. Boy, would that be awkward. We have some great romantic music queued up, Frank Sinatra and the other boys from the Rat Pack. If you are too young for that reference, google it.

Alan and I will welcome them at 6:00 p.m. and introduce ourselves and set the weekend up before the servers start bringing out their meals. We had them select their meal choices when they registered to save time and make sure everyone had a full and satisfied tummy. After dinner, we'll have dessert, a great tiramisu with coffee or wine. We'll do some mingling before turning in for the evening, so we are well rested for tomorrow's activities.

I look at my watch, 5:55 p.m., and here comes our first couple for dinner.

"Mr. and Mrs. Reynolds! How lovely to see you. I can't begin to tell you how excited I am that you are part of this weekend," I exclaim with very real and raw emotion.

"Thank you, Kate, we are pleased as punch to have been able to make it happen. We figured another visit to see Benji at school would be perfect to have coincide with this marriage weekend. I can't tell you how we need this. Margaret had dropped her babies with us for a full two weeks to go off on holiday with her husband, which we were obviously pleased to do, but between that and Rose finishing secondary school in a few months, we needed this. It will be so nice to be just us for a few days," Mrs. Reynolds replied.

As I show Mr. and Mrs. Reynolds to their table, two other couples enter the dining room. The Mertzs and the Clooneys. Mr. and Mrs. Mertz are an older couple who have struggled for years with infertility, and it has taken a toll on their relationship. Sadly, you can see it in their faces. I send up a silent prayer for them as they are shown their table by one of the servers, "Lord, please meet the Mertzs this weekend and restore their hope and their love for one another."

I spot Alan walking in along with the last two couples, the Reeds and the Garcias. As the couples make their ways to their tables, Alan greets me with a quick kiss on the cheek.

"Are we good?" I ask.

"Absolutely, I love you, Kate. Listen, it's not surprising we got into it the morning that we are hosting a marriage retreat. We are humans. Sometimes even the best of us falls short." He winks at me. "Now let's go rock this marriage retreat!"

I grab his hand as we step up to the mic to start our very first marriage retreat weekend. This morning, I woke up a bit frantic, my weakness, as you may or may not have surmised by now, is control. I like to be in control, to have control, especially when I feel like things are out of control. In those circumstances, one might say I tend to have "no chill." So with everything piling up and facing the weight and beauty of being able to lead five other couples for a whole weekend, I freaked. I exploded at Alan and accused him of being no help and said some hurtful and unnecessary things. It took a good portion of our morning, nevertheless after some brave communication—a topic we teach on at our weekend—irony, followed by me asking for forgiveness, we were able to move forward and work as a team to see this marriage retreat happen.

"Welcome, lovers, to our very first marriage retreat at Still Waters Inn! We are so excited that you have all agreed to be part of our beta group for this—hopefully the first of many—marriage retreat. Our prayer for this weekend is that you will have some meaningful connection time with your spouse and leave feeling hopeful and excited for your journey as husband and wife.

"Kate and I have trained, prayed, and lived ups and downs of marriage to prepare for this weekend. We are excited to share with you what we've learned and what we try to implement in our own marriage. We've sent you an itinerary for the weekend in your email after you registered, so hopefully you've all had a chance to look it over before coming here tonight. Of course, the ever-thorough Kate has also included a printed copy of our itinerary in each of your rooms with your welcome basket," adds Alan.

"Now let's pray before the servers start bringing out your dinners. Dear Lord, we thank You for this weekend and bringing these precious couples together this weekend to grow in their relationship with You and each other. Thank You for this delicious dinner, bless it to our bodies and bless the hands that prepared it and let us be a blessing to one another and to You. In Jesus's name. Amen."

Just as I finish praying, the servers start bringing out the guest meals. The guest couldn't help but enjoy their dinner. Nikki is an absolute wizard with Italian cuisine, and tonight she shined in the kitchen. As the guest finish their meals, Nikki pokes her head out of the kitchen and waves me back.

"What's up, Nikki? Everyone loved their meals. They were ranting and raving as they were shoveling." I laugh as I come into the kitchen.

"It's the tiramisu…" Nikki mumbled nervously. "It's dead. Grab a shovel, and we can take it out back and hold a funeral, but it is dead, and there ain't no resurrecting it. I don't know what to do. I don't have anything else to serve them for dessert! They were promised tiramisu, and I've failed them. I've failed you!"

I'm torn; part of me wants to join in the freak out and go ballistic right alongside Nikki about the absolute disaster this is, but on the other hand, I feel the responsibility as the owner to defuse the situation and find a solution or, as Alan calls it, "put out the fire."

I take a deep breath. "Nikki, breathe with me. It will be okay. We will figure it out."

"Let's see." I start opening cupboards and the fridge to see what can be done. "We've got to have something. It's too bad Jessica hasn't had time to bake for the inn right now with finals and everything."

Just then, Alan comes in, and Nikki and I explain everything to him.

"Well," Alan says, "I could go for some chocolate. Do we have any bars or candies?"

"Alan, that's it!" I exclaim. "We have that box of Toblerones! We can serve those to them in a pinch, and I'd say this is a pinch. Nikki, is the coffee going?"

"Freshly brewed, regular, and decaf, and I've opened some bottles of wine so they can breathe," Nikki responds.

"Perfect, well, Alan let's go break the news." Alan grabs my hand, and we leave the kitchen and head into the dining room.

Alan clears his throat to get the room's attention.

"Hi, everyone, it appears that the original dessert for this evening, tiramisu, will not be available and will be replaced with your very own bar of Toblerone. The servers will also be coming by with coffee and wine as well if you so desire. Please enjoy."

Alan nods at me his approval. "You handled that very nicely. I'm proud of you, babe."

"Thank you. Of course, you are the problem-solver extraordinaire. I'm lucky to be your wife."

"I love you," Alan says.

"I love you too," I respond.

* * * * *

Marriage Weekend
Saturday Morning Itinerary

8:00 a.m.	Breakfast in the dining room: Your choice of eggs benedict, French toast avocado toast or yogurt parfait
9:00 a.m.	Husbands only with Alan
10:00 a.m.	Kayaking or floating the Sacramento River
12:00–3:00 p.m.	Free time
3:00 p.m.	Brave communication
4:30 p.m.	Games in the community room
6:00 p.m.	Picnic dinner under the stars

"Good morning, Kate!" call out the Mertzs as they grab their table for breakfast.

"Good morning, Fred and Ethel! I hope you had a good night sleep."

"We did, thank you! We always love staying at Still Waters, and what a gift to be able to invest in our marriage as well," Ethel says.

"I'm so glad to hear that. We are honored you are here with us," I reply.

"Kate, we plan on staying an extra night or two after the marriage retreat, and we were wondering if we could have dinner with you and Alan—just the four of us—before we head out," Ethel asks.

"We would love to let me run it by Alan and check our calendar, and I'll let you know this afternoon."

"Sounds good! We are looking forward to the picnic under the stars tonight," Ethel says dreamily.

"Have a good breakfast you two!" I wave as I walk out of the dining room and walk past the room Alan is going to do his "husbands-only class." Look how cute he looks in there prepping for his talk. Like he needs much prep, Alan has always been such a natural in the realm of public speaking. I can't wait to hear his feedback on our kayak ride later.

* * * * *

"How do you feel your husbands-only session went, babe?" I ask as Alan and I get in our kayak.

"It went great! The guys were all interactive and asked a lot of good questions. I feel good about this group. We talked about taking ownership of how we treat our wives and asking questions like, Does she feel protected? We graded ourselves as husbands and had honest conversations about how we can grow," Alan answered enthusiastically.

"I'm so proud of you, Alan," I say as I row.

"I am so glad that we planned this kayaking time. It's a treat that you and I get to steal away and have some romantic fun!"

"Oh, before I forget, the Mertz's would like to have dinner with us after the conference. They plan on staying an extra night or two. Do we have anything planned those days?" I inquire.

"Nope, we have it free until Wednesday when we are meeting with Donald." Alan double-checks the calendar on his phone.

Just then my cell phone goes off.

"Hello?" I answer.

"Kate, you must come quickly! The inn is flooding! And call the plumber," replies Mitchell through the phone.

"Mitchell, we are in the middle of the Sacramento River. I will call the plumber and try to meet them there, but it's going to take us a little bit to get back to shore. Do me a favor, Mitchell, take a deep breath and tell me the details. Where is it? What's the damage situation, etc.? Also, where is Doug? Has he already looked at it?" I try to reply calmly.

Mitchell takes a deep breath. "Doug is here, and he is turning off the water right now, but he said it's outside his paygrade. Please hurry, Kate!"

I hang up and fill Alan in as we maneuver our kayak and start rowing back to shore. Thankfully, I have the plumber, Ian, in my contacts, and I can call him from my Apple Watch, so I don't have to stop rowing. I am going to be sore tomorrow.

"Siri, call Ian, the plumber."

3

"Thanks for coming so quickly, Ian."

"No problem, Kate. I'll get my guys in here to take care of this for you, and then we will assess the damage and try to do it as quickly as we can without interfering with your guest," Ian replies as he jots something down on his clipboard.

"It looks like you've got a busted pipe in the guest bathroom that's causing the issue. The water is shut off, so Tom can fix it, and hopefully we can get ahead of the water damage. It's a good thing you don't serve dinner, and you may even need to serve breakfast on the patio in the morning."

"We actually are doing a marriage retreat at the inn this weekend, and we are serving dinner, but tonight we are doing dinner picnic style outside."

"Sounds good. I'll go check in with Tom and go check out the floors in the dining room. It looks like my guys almost have the dining room completely cleared out."

As Ian walks away, I turn to Alan. "Oh my gosh, I can't believe this is happening! This of all weekends! Thankfully Ian and his team were able to come out on a Saturday, but this is bonkers!"

"It's going to be okay, Kate. Everything will work out, and this will just be a small blip in our lives." Alan calmly reassures me as he holds my arms in his hands.

I fall into his arms and try to find comfort in his embrace. How quickly those taunting voices come back and lies worm their way in—things like "failure" or "this is what I get for trying something out of my comfort zone" or "the sky is falling" or "everybody hates me, nobody likes me, I'll just go eat some worms," and so on and so forth.

Alan pulls me out to arm's length. "Kate, look at me. Stuff happens. We can't control the outcome of every situation. All we can do is trust God, keep our eyes fixed on Him, and not listen to the negativity that tries to come in and weigh us down. It takes our gaze off Him, distracts us from our purpose, and you and I are doing a really cool thing here. This marriage retreat is something that we've been dreaming of and planning for years."

Ian comes back in the room. "I'm so sorry, Kate, the floors are completely warped, and we are going to have to rip them out, dry the area thoroughly, and lay down all new flooring."

* * * * *

Marriage Weekend
Sunday/Valentine's Day Itinerary

8:00 a.m.	~~Pancake breakfast with berries and bacon~~ Muffins and coffee on the porch
9:00 a.m.	Worship and devotionals ~~in the foyer~~ under the Gazebo
10:30–12:00 p.m.	Kate and Alan teach brave communication
12:00–5:00 p.m.	Free time
5:00 p.m.	~~Valentine's dinner and dance~~ BBQ and dance on the lawn
9:00 p.m.	Farewell

"Muffins and coffee are all set up on the porch, Kate," Nikki announces.

"Perfect! Thank you so much, Nikki. I couldn't do any of this without you, but of course, you already know that," I reply. I need to make sure Nikki knows just how valuable she is to this inn and to me.

"Hon, you've got nothing to worry about. You were born to run an inn. Plus, once the guests taste my special raspberry muffins with a crumble topping, they will forget all the chaos happening in the dining room right now," says Nikki matter-of-factly.

"I called Roxy and Simone as well, so we have backup for tonight's BBQ and outdoor dance. They are bringing supplies and their husbands so they can turn a work night into a date night. LOL. Is Jack coming tonight? I know you, guys, were looking for a sitter so he could join."

"He said he is. Our sitter committed, so we should be good to go, and he's gonna help me with the grill," Nikki said. You could see the relief and excitement as she talked about her husband joining us for the Valentine's BBQ and dance tonight.

"Did Ian give you a time frame for how long the repairs will take yet?" Nikki asks.

"Not yet. Ian is ordering the floors today, and then once he gets an ETA for delivery, he said he will be able to give me a more realistic time frame. I'm trying not to think about it too much. I just want to get through today and hopefully salvage what's left of our marriage retreat."

"Here comes your first guest for breakfast. I'll go make sure I keep the coffee coming," Nikki says as she runs around back to the kitchen.

"Good morning and happy Valentine's Day, Mr. and Mrs. Clooney. I hope you slept well. I apologize for the mess in the dining room and having to switch our itinerary a bit for today."

"Good morning, Kate, don't worry about a thing. Everything here is lovely. We slept great, and we are so excited for today! And please call us Tim and Isla. Can I talk to for a minute alone, Kate?"

"Sure, Isla."

A million things are now running through my head. What complaints does she have for me? I'm sure I'll have to refund the whole weekend. This is a disaster!

"Kate, I'd like to pray for you and encourage you really quick if that's all right."

"Isla, I would love that. Wow! Thank you!"

"Jesus, would You come and be with my beautiful new friend, Kate, right now. Fill her day with fun and peace and let her rest in You, knowing You have got her in the palm of Your hand. Thank You for this weekend and for the faithfulness of Kate and Alan to do what You've placed on their heart to do and minister to and pour into other marriages. Bless them and their inn in Jesus's name. Amen," Isla prayed.

"Wow, Isla, I'm so blessed. Thank you," I respond.

"Kate, what you and Alan are doing here is truly beautiful, and Tim and I are getting so much out of this weekend, as are the other couples, I'm sure. You've really lavished us with your sweet atmosphere, wisdom, peace, and the presence of God. This is a priceless gift, and you have to keep going," Isla encouraged.

Just then, Alan and the rest of the guest join them on the porch.

"Good morning and happy Valentine's Day, everyone! Thank you for your grace and understanding with what's going on at the inn right now and understanding its completely out of our hands, and we are doing everything in our power to ensure your last day here with us is wonderful. Thankfully we have been blessed with good weather today, so moving all the activities outdoors should be very pleasant. If you have any questions or concerns at all, please feel free to ask me or Alan. I've placed update itineraries for today by the coffee and muffins, so be sure to grab one along with your breakfast. Once you have finished your breakfast, feel free to join us under the gazebo for a time of worship and devotionals."

"Hey, babe!" Alan says as he gives me a quick kiss. "I'm going to take my guitar over to the gazebo and tune. Would you be a doll and bring me some coffee and one of those delicious muffins?"

"Sure, I'm just about finished over here, and I'll be over in a few to warm up with you," I respond.

As I walked over to grab Alan some coffee, I quietly sent up a prayer of gratitude, "God, I'm thankful that You are taking care of us, the inn, and this retreat. I'm thankful to be able to lead with my husband and worship You together this morning. I'm thankful that

I can always count on You because You are faithful. Thank You for being a good Father. Amen."

* * * * *

Brave Communication Taught by Alan and Kate Brown

After I shared a brief overview of brave communication and, of course, a handout with bullet points, we segued into talking about love languages.

Alan got up to share and started with one of our favorite stories to tell. "Who wants to hear about Alan and Kate's early dating woes? Raise your hand and wave it at me!"

Everyone followed the instructions and waved at Alan. I rolled my eyes, I always thought that was so cheesy, but he loved doing it.

He continued, "When Kate and I were dating, I would walk into her house, and when she was getting ready to go, I would do her dishes. In my mind, I was being a great boyfriend to her by helping out around the house. I didn't get the 'thank-yous' I was expecting all the time, but I felt like I was really doing a good job. Well, Kate would bring me these little gifts. A candy bar here or a small doodad there, and I just didn't get it. I even told her one day, 'Why do you waste your money on this stuff? I don't get it!'"

There was an audible gasp in the room as he closed out his story. They couldn't believe that Alan told me I was wasting my money buying him gifts! When he's speaking, he feeds on the reactions of the audience, and I could tell his energy levels were going up...even though the audience wasn't really on his side at this point.

Alan asked the room, "Do you know why I was washing the dishes? To show Kate that I love and appreciate her, and why was she buying me gifts? *Love languages!*"

I knew he was in his element when he yelled during his speech. I smiled watching him, and I could see from his facial expression that he was in his groove.

"Who has taken the love languages test? Raise your hand!" Alan prompted the audience, and only one or two couples raised their hands.

Alan went on to explain the five love languages and how I was speaking love in *gifts*, and he was speaking love in "acts of service."

Alan ended his talk by showing everyone how to take the test from their phones and discover their own love languages and the love language of their spouse.

"All right, that's enough for now everyone. Go to your rooms, kiss for a few minutes, and see what happens!" Alan said with a wink.

The room laughed, and all the couples rushed to their rooms to talk about their love language's test I was sure.

"Okay, Alan!" I got up to close out our session and saved Alan from "going there." "Have a great afternoon, everyone, and we will see you this evening for a yummy BBQ dinner and a romantic evening of dancing under the stars."

As everyone started filtering out, Alan and I started cleaning up the gazebo and debriefing about how we felt the class went.

"That was so fun, babe. I love the way we play off each other, even if you do get a little risqué every now and then." I laughed.

"Awe, you love it! And I love to get a rise out of you. But, yes, we do make a great team, Kate. We always have, and we always will. This is just the beginning for our marriage ministry. I really feel that. You and I are called to pour into other marriages," Alan said with sincerity.

"I love you, Alan."

"I love you too, Kate."

* * * * *

My Clumsy Valentine

Valentine's Day, the day of hearts and flowers, the day of romance, love, and intimacy. The day when, if you're safely ensconced in a relationship, you are full of joy and basking in the surprise of the displays of affection from your man. However, sometimes even if you are in a relationship, it can be hard and end in heartache and disappointment. The goal of today's portion and more specifically tonight's dinner/dance was to take the pressure off.

When the couples booked their retreat, we gave specific instructions: "This year, no flowers, no chocolates, no elaborate gifts or gestures. The gift this year is investing in your marriage. Let us bring the gifts, and you focus on each other and your emotional needs. As I walk around the grounds, admiring the twinkle lights strung through the trees and the pink and red roses almost enveloping the outside of the gazebo, I was hopeful, and I sent up a prayer to the Lord, not just for a successful event, but that these couples would leave here changed. That they would have fallen deeper in love with their spouse and that they would leave here with a renewed sense of hope for the future and a refined sense of commitment to the life they share as two people who have been unified as one.

The table and chairs have been set up intentionally—two settings only. Dinner will be intimate. Well, as intimate as a BBQ can be. I have the waiters in white button ups and a black tie tonight to give it a more formal flare. The tables have white tablecloths and a single gold candlestick and white taper candle, wine glasses with red cloth napkins. Each guest was delivered red roses to their room earlier this afternoon. Nikki and Jack have tri tip, salmon, potatoes, and veggies going on the grill. Of course, they will be served my famous strawberry, blueberry, spinach salad with candied pecans and poppy seed dressing first, then their main course, followed by their choice of devil's food cake with cholate ganache or NY cheesecake top with cherries.

"Kate, how do I look?" Simone asked as she twirled her flouncy black dress, trying to steady herself on her sparkly pumps.

"Oh, Simone, you look gorgeous! Did Chad see you before you came out here looking like that?" I asked and gave a low whistle.

Simone blushed, "Yes, he did. I think it's safe to say he likes the way I look." She giggled.

"Oh good! You're both here. I need some serious assistance guys." Roxy came barreling out, looking a bit disheveled.

"Roxy, what happened to you?" I asked.

"The kids almost didn't let me out the door. I'm telling you they are going to put me in an early grave. Come on ladies, into the lady's room. I need assistance—stat!"

"We are coming!" Simone and I said in unison as we followed her into the inn.

Roxy unzipped her garment bag and pulled out a stunning vintage pinup style black halter dress with cherries. She paired it with some black wedges and a sweet rose gold necklace and earrings set. Simone added a red rose placed strategically in her hair as Simone finished curling Roxy's hair. I touched up her makeup and voila! She, too, was stunning!

In case you're wondering what I was wearing, you'd be right if you guessed my red Kate Spade swing dress with black strappy low heels. (Remember, I'm already quite tall.) My long red hair in loose wavy curls and, of course, red lipstick was a must for Valentine's evening.

"Ladies, I don't think our men are going to survive the night," I said half-jokingly.

Just then there was a knock at the bathroom door.

"Kate? Simone? Roxy? Are you guys in there?" Alan asked.

"Yes!" we responded in unison, looking at each other sheepishly.

"It's time to get started, ladies. Are you ready? Simone and Roxy, your husbands Chad and Bruce are looking a little lost without you. You can't make a man dress up and leave him to fend for himself." Alan laughed as we opened the door and filtered out.

"All right, let's do this!" I say with anticipation for a great evening.

Dinner went off without a hitch like usual Nikki and Jack made Michelin-level BBQ and deserts. The guests were all happily fed, and the DJ we hired started getting people on the dance floor we rented for the evening in an effort to avoid ladies' heels from getting stuck in the grass.

As I go about from table to table, making sure everything was tidy while the guests were dancing, Alan walked over to me.

"Can I have the last dance, pretty lady?" he asked.

"Sure, sounds great." Just then I heard what song started playing; it was Harry Connick Jr. singing "It Had to Be You." Swoon! Am I in for a heart full of emotions.

One of my favorite things is slow dancing to crooner music with Alan. We don't do it often, but when we do, my knees would turn to jelly.

Alan put his arms around my waist, and I put my hands around his neck. It's really more of a hug and sway to the music than a dance. As we glided across the dance floor and enjoyed being in each other's arms, I let myself be carried away by the ambience and the silky smooth rumblings of Harry Connick Jr.'s voice. I've read that when you dance, your body releases endorphins, the chemical that triggers positive energy and good vibes. I think it's safe to say this was the perfect way to end the weekend.

As the song comes to a close, Alan and I scurried off the dance floor, grabbed a glass of wine, and headed up the steps of the gazebo.

"Attention, everyone!" Alan boomed as the music ends.

Everyone stopped dancing and shifted their attention toward us.

"We want to end our evening and officially end our very first marriage retreat brought to you by Still Waters Inn by giving a toast. Everyone, please grab a glass. There are wine glasses with both wine and sparkling cider if you prefer on the table behind you."

The crowd noisily went to collect their glasses and joined back together in front of the gazebo as I gave a toast.

"Here is to all of you, each one is here because of the love you have for your spouse, your commitment to each other, and to the growth and health of your marriage. You have not only invested in your marriage this weekend, but also you've invested into your legacy. You will leave this legacy for future generations who can build upon what you've cultivated her this weekend. So as we cheers in a few minutes, we solidify all the ground that was gained her this weekend, and we walk forward in victory full of hope for the future and equipped to build healthy happy homes till death do us both part. May the Lord bless you and keep you. May His face shine upon you and be gracious to you. May the Lord turn His face toward you and give you peace. Amen. *Cheers!*"

As everyone clinked their glasses in cheers and takes a sip, I turned toward Alan to clink his glass with mine when my strappy heel caught on an extension cord, and I stumbled throwing my *red wine* all over Alan's white crisp button-up shirt. I gasped in horror as I felt myself about to tumble down the steps. Just then, I felt Alan's strong arms catch me and hoist me up. I slipped my heel off my foot and caught my balance.

"I've got you, Kate, my clumsy Valentine."

4

We did it! We made it through Valentine's weekend and our first marriage retreat/weekend with only slight damage. Now to focus on getting the inn back up and running. Oh yeah, we had to close temporarily until the floors get replaced and all the water damage was out. I didn't realize there would be monster fans and humidifiers and giant plastic tarps taping off multiple areas of the inn to dry the space out. There was just no way we could have guest here while this was going on, not to mention the noise of them ripping the old flooring out of the dining room. Luckily that was the "quick" part. I had to issue a few refunds, which hurt my heart, but I'm determined to not let this steal my joy or my focus.

We were on our way to meet Fred and Ethel Mertz for dinner at our favorite local Thai restaurant.

"Hi, guys!" I greeted the Mertzs as we walked into the restaurant.

They were already at a table for four, so they waved us over to join them.

"Thank you so much for making time for us after everything going on with the inn," Fred said.

"You're welcome, truth be told this is a welcome distraction." Alan responds.

"So I have to ask. How was the marriage retreat for you two? I'd love some honest feedback," I asked.

"We loved it. I believe we are going home with new tools, and we are excited to grow our marriage. It was triggering at times, especially being the only ones there not able to have children." Ethel explained. "That is why we wanted to speak to you guys privately, we wanted you to be the first to know."

Ethel looked like she was going to burst with excitement, and I was equally anxious to hear their news.

"After our talk when we stayed here at the Inn last year, Fred and I followed your advice and pursued adopting through foster care. We finished our certification two weeks ago, and on our way to Still Water, we got a call from the agency, and we got matched with a baby. We wanted to take you and Alan out and personally thank you. If it hadn't been for your prayers and encouragement, we would have never even considered this path and wouldn't be about to meet our new foster son. Our prayers have been answered, and our family is growing! We can't tell you enough how grateful we are for you, your prayers, and Still Waters Inn. The inn has been a place of solace and life bringing hope when we've needed it the most. On next time we stay, it will be three instead of two."

"Alan and I are so happy for you and your growing family, and if you need anything, please do not hesitate to give us a call. You are always in our prayers, and we can't wait to meet the newest member of your family!"

In awe of what God's done for the Mertzs, I can't help but have my perspective shifted. This is what it's about, seeing people get their miracle, providing a place of hope, peace, and comfort. Still Waters is more than just an ordinary inn. It's a true place of restoration and rejuvenation, not just for your physical body but for your spiritual and emotional health as well. This is why this makes everything worth it. I am so thankful. So my floors were a mess, and I had to cancel a few (or more) reservations, this was small potatoes in the grand scheme of things. A blip, a hiccup. Like Alan said, this too shall pass. Not only that, but I also get to open a second location. A double portion! Thank God for Your goodness and Your faithfulness.

* * * * *

I'm on my way right now to a planning meeting with Alan and Donald to talk about locations for our new inn. Dreaming is good medicine for the soul. There was a time in my life where dreaming only happened at night, and it was usually a nightmare. The Lord took me through a process of discovering the joy of dreaming and doing it with Him. Dreaming with God is so much more satisfying than anything I could ever dream on my own, not only is God more creative than me but He also always knows the better way. Here are nine of my favorite scriptures that encourage me when I get off track from pursuing my dreams. I hope they will bless you as much as they bless me.

> For I know the plans I have for you," declares the Lord, "plans to prosper you and not to harm you, plans to give you a hope and a future. (Jeremiah 29:11)

> But seek first His kingdom and His righteousness, and all these things will be given to you. (Matthew 6:33)

> Commit to the Lord whatever you do, and He will establish your plans. (Proverbs 16:3)

> I can do all things through Him who gives me strength. (Philippians 4:13)

> I will repay you for the years the locust have eaten… (Joel 2:25)

> Then the Lord replied: "Write down the revelation and make it plain on tablets so that a herald may run with it." (Habakkuk 2:2)

> Do not be anxious about anything, but in every situation, by prayer and petition, with

thanksgiving, present your request to God. (Philippians 4:6)

A gift opens the way and usher the giver into the presence of the great. (Proverbs 18:16)

Being confident of this, that He who began a good work in you will carry it on to completion until the day of Christ Jesus. (Philippians 1:6)

* * * * *

"Hey, babe, good morning, Donald," I say as I join them in the booth of our favorite diner.

"Good morning, Kate, I'm so sorry to hear about Stillwater. What's the verdict?" Donald asks.

"I spoke to Ian this morning, and the plumbing problems have all been fixed. Praise God! They have ripped out the warped flooring in the dining room and has ordered the new floors. The company gave them and Eta of next Monday, but he said everything has been on back order so not to be too surprised if it comes later. They have the big old fans going to dry out all the moisture and water/damage, and we've canceled all reservations for the next two weeks," I reply with a big sigh.

"You know, Kate, I know this all looks really bad right now, and I can see you are discouraged, but this may be just a blessing in disguise," Donald says.

I gawk at him with wide eyes blinking just waiting to hear the punch line. Surely, he can't be serious.

"Now hear me out, starting another inn is a lot of work, right? You haven't completely stepped away from running Still Waters yet. Now you have two weeks to completely devote to getting your new inn. Have you thought of a name yet?"

"You have a good point, Donald, that is a more positive way to think about it. I can have Mitchell and Nikki overlook the rest of the repairs so I can focus more on 'No Name Inn.'" I laugh as I respond.

"See, Kate?" Alan says enthusiastically, "This is why I love Donald, so glad to have you part of the team man!"

"Thanks, Alan, we better get off this love fest cruise and start some actual work. Here are five properties I've found for us to look at. I want to go over each one with you, and we can plan our trip to go check them out. Since Kate is not going to be tied to Still Waters for the next two weeks, I can book us flights for this weekend. Are you, folks, ready for New York?"

Donald, who has an extremely deadpan and stereotypical masculine personality actively, tries to convince those around him of his hard exterior—it's most effective in the business and finance world to get him closing deals, but occasionally you can catch a glimpse of the giant teddy bear that is really is, compassionate and caring, one of the most generous humans I've encountered. He loves meat, woodworking, hunting, whiskey, breakfast foods, and nautical literature. He also loves the Lord and is a man after God's own heart.

"Looks like we are going to New York this weekend!" I say. "Let me just call Jessica and make sure she is good to watch after Molly while she's studying for finals."

"Tell her congratulations for me for getting into Cal Poly. I hear they have a great film program," Donald adds.

"She's always wanted to live near the beach, she is stoked!" replies Alan.

After a quick call to Jessica to let her know our plans and to make sure she can indeed watch my little bichon frise, Molly, we pour over the five properties Donald brought in and in true type A fashion I make a list of pros and cons for each of them. We were able to narrow it down to two. One in Alexandria Bay and one in Ithaca.

The city of Ithaca is widely known for stunning natural beauty and thriving local culture. They boast one-of-a-kind restaurants, galleries, and live music events. You can explore nearby gorges and shores of Cayuga Lake. Tons of tourist means successful Inn.

Alexandria Bay is a charming village in upstate New York, part of the Thousand Islands (yes, just like the salad dressing—Alan's favorite). A four-season destination ($$$$$) filled with stunning natural beauty, intriguing history, outdoor adventures, and some of the best fishing in the US! They boast castles and cruises, outdoor fun and a winery.

By the end of our meeting, I'm eager to get packing and fly out in two days to look at both properties. Maybe if one of these is a winner, the name of my new inn will come to me.

* * * * *

As I'm finishing packing mine and Alan's mostly packed suitcases for our week in New York, I'm hit again with something that resembles the feeling of grief. I look around our beautiful master bedroom at the decor that I thoughtfully and meticulously chose to be a sanctuary and a place of retreat, rest, and romance. The gorgeous muted blue-green paint color that Alan hired someone to paint as a birthday present to me, I feel a pang of pain in my heart know that I'll be leaving this treasured place for who knows how long. I'm choosing to trust God. I know His plans for me are good and that this is a continuation of seeing my dreams come true, yet it's still hard to say goodbye, even if it's "for now."

As I zip up our suitcases, little Molly gives me a look of disapproval. Firstly, she thinks those full, open suitcases made a lovely nap spot. Secondly, in her old age, her separation anxiety has gotten pretty bad. I usually take her everywhere with me, but traveling to a new place by plane doesn't seem like the best place to take my seven-pound elderly white poufy little bichon frise.

"Hey, Mom!" Jessica zips in, scooping Molly up in her arms, and plops down on my bed where the suitcases previously resided.

"What's up, Jess?" I inquire, giving her my full attention, knowing these times when she seeks me out to chat are rare and extremely valuable.

"I am burned-out. How am I supposed to take these finals? I can't even think about Cal Poly right now. More school seems like a nightmare and a punishment right now. Even if I'll be studying what I love, I'm just…done!" Jessica states as she grabs my pillow, wraps her arms around it, and tucks her chin into the top of it.

"I'm sorry, hon, I know you have been working so hard studying and putting in the work, but I promise you it will be worth it. Finals are not even that soon, give yourself a breather. You don't have to even think about college right now. Just take it one day at a time, do your best, and let everything else go. Maybe tonight you can have a girlfriend over for some self-care time? Give yourself a brain break," I advise.

"That's a good idea, Mom, a pint of chocolate cookie dough ice cream and a *Harry Potter* marathon sound like the perfect medicine," Jessica says. "I've been thinking about prom too. I'm not sure I want to go."

"Why is that, honey? Aren't your friends going?" I ask, my curiosity piqued.

"Well, yeah, but they already have dates. Rory is going with her boyfriend Dean and Lane is going with Logan. I don't want to be a fifth wheel." Jessica moped.

"Are you still missing Nick?" I ask gently. I don't want to push too much and spook my teenager just as she's opening up.

Her brief relationship with her ex-boyfriend Nick spanned over a few months during the summer and ended when his family moved to New Jersey, and he didn't want to have a long-distance girlfriend. It has broken Jessica's young heart. But since Christmas, she seemed to be on the upswing, smiling more, going out with her friends, and having fun. I'm suspecting that with the stress of the end of her high school career and a solo prom season looming in her face, it's brought up some of those lingering wounds.

"Probably," Jessica responds hesitantly. "I mean, I thought we'd be together forever. I thought that we'd go to senior prom together and finish high school together, but he just left. I know his family had to move, and so he had to go with them, but he didn't even want to try dating long distance," she said with a sniffle.

"Did *you* want to have a long-distance relationship during your senior year of high school?" I ask.

"Well…no, of course not! I wanted him to stay. I wanted to go to open our college acceptance letters together, I wanted to go to senior prom together, and I wanted to graduate together, go to college together. I loved him, I think," Jessica said thoughtfully.

"I know, honey, I'm so sorry your hurting," I say as I rub your back. "I have a few hours before we have to leave for the airport. You want to go get some ice cream?"

"That sounds great! Thanks, Mom." Jessica dries her tears and goes to grab her shoes.

I've learned on this journey of motherhood that I've still got a lot to learn. Haha, got ya! No, but really, I've also learned that sometimes I need to put my to-do list down and create space to provide a safe landing space, especially in the teen years. Most of the time, she craves her independence, and for the most part, she doesn't seem to need me much anymore. But when she does, I'm here, and she is my priority. Motherhood is a gift, and one I will never take for granted.

I've been blessed to have done a lot of things in my life that are really cool, but none am I as proud of or has brought me as much joy as Jessica.

You're probably thinking, *Whoa, sappy parent moment! Where did that come from?* To that, I say, "It's my story. Ha! Also, fourth wall what? Oh yeah, I broke that a long time ago."

I think we are all ready for chapter 5 now.

5

Friday, we arrived at Albany International Airport around noon. It was an early flight for us especially with the three-hour time difference. But we all three are running on adrenaline and very excited to see these properties. Today we see the inn in Ithaca, and tomorrow we head to Alexandria Bay. We grab our rental car, and after a three-hour drive, we arrive in Ithaca and drive through town to the address given to us by our realtor down a quaint floral-lined street full of cute little shops, boutiques, and mom-and-pop kitchens.

I start daydreaming about our inn in Ithaca. The alliteration is a bit much, but the town is dreamy! It's still a bit brisk outside, but it's a gorgeous sunny day, and if you didn't know any better, you'd think it was spring already, looking for people walking around in sundresses and short-sleeve T-shirts but the town folks, where donning light jackets to protect from the last remnants of winter.

We pull into the winding driveway of a beautiful white three-story Victorian Inn with a wraparound porch. We walk up the steps of the front porch, and our realtor is there to meet us.

"Hi, I'm Paul. It's nice to finally meet you all in person," Paul says as he shakes Alan and my hands.

"Hi, Donald, good to see you again!" Paul says as he shakes Donald's hand. "Are you, folks, ready to see some beautiful properties?"

"Yes!" I reply enthusiastically as I take in the front archway. We are about to walk under to get to the front door that has been freshly painted crimson red.

Paul enters a code into the door, and it unlocks. It's a smart inn. Love that. We walk into the foyer, and it's a high ceiling with a huge chandelier. There is an archway to my right and to my left and a staircase in front of me. To the right, Paul lets us know this is the sitting area/library. It's dark, warm, and cozy. The walls are lined with bookcase except for the wall with the fireplace and a big window looking out to the old oak tree in the side yard.

There are three different seating areas in clusters throughout the room. A big plushy love seat facing the fireplace and the other two consist of giant oversized armchairs facing each other with a side table by each. Each seating area has a basket of cozy blankets next to them so the guest can cozy up while they relax and/or read. I can instantly picture people sitting by the fire curled up with a book and a cup of hot chocolate and a snowy winter wonderland outside the window.

The tour continues while my daydreams dance through my mind. Paul takes us through the archway to the left, where there is a reception desk for guest to check in and collect their room code, as it's a smart inn, and there is no physical key. The desk itself is a tall cherrywood, and behind it is a huge oil painting of a serene lake, which Paul informs us is Cayuga Lake that runs right through Ithaca.

Through the hall past the reception desk, we come into the dining room that has eight tiny tables with two chairs each. To the left of the dining room are swinging double doors that lead into the kitchen, which is a full commercial kitchen, and I am overwhelmed just stepping foot in there, thinking of all the hungry people to be fed from this kitchen. Huge industrial stainless-steel appliances, a walk-in fridge, and ample counter space. A chefs dream, I'm sure. The kitchen has a back door that goes out to the back patio, down the steps is an herb garden. Beyond is a sprawling green lawn littered with kitschy outdoor furniture.

After we go inside and check out all the bedrooms and finish our tour, I am beyond wiped. Alan, Doug, and I agree it's a grab, a quick dinner to go, and head to our hotel so we can get a good-night sleep before we head to Alexandria Bay in the morning. I'm sure you're wondering what I thought of the Ithaca Inn, but I think I'll make you wait until I see Alexandria Bay's Inn. I mean, what's this chapter without a good pros and con's list?

* * * * *

Alexandria Bay

After a quick continental breakfast at our hotel, we star our two-and-a-half-hour drive to Alexandria Bay. The drive through upstate New York is breathtaking. I'm not even sure saying it was a "scenic view" does it justice. We head straight to the property to meet our realtor, Paul.

We drive up to this very cute and old Victorian (it's a must for any inn to be in a Victorian-style house, come on). In the front, there is a huge sign "Something Inn," the name of the inn has been covered by a "for sale" sign. The inn is a creamy off-white freshly painted with a dark-teal trim. Wraparound porch (also a must) with huge bay windows. The second floor has one of those pop out rooms with a mini steeple that make it look like a tiny castle. Rocking chairs litter the porch and the walkway leading to the porch has an arch covered in wisteria, such a heavenly smell. Once you walk through the archway, there is a sweet little sign that says "entrance" with an arrow pointing the front door. The walk is lined with well-manicured shrubs. The front yard looks like something out of *The Secret Garden*.

The front door is a heavy cherrywood, next to the front door hangs a heavy iron sign that says "Historic Davis House" with the house number under. I remember Paul sending us a brief history of this place; it's been preserved by the historic foundation. The first settlement located in Alexandria Bay was around 1811. The Town of Alexandria Bay was established in 1821 from the town of Brownsville and the Town of LeRay. The battle of Cranberry Creek, a battle that took place in the war of 1812, is a big part of the town's history. The original owner of this house was Elijah Davis who kept a tavern inn. The Davis house served as a meeting place for the militia officers due to its central location and spacious meeting rooms. It has since been renovated, but it has good solid bones for being around since the 1800s.

The inside is pretty standard as far as inn's go, the kitchen much meeker than the last, although still good in size. The six bedrooms all have private baths, and in the attic is an indoor hot tub and sauna that the previous owner installed. I was much more excited to see the backyard after the teaser of the front of the property. It did not disappoint. We walk out the French doors adjoining the library/sitting room to the back porch, crawling ivy covered the railing. The steps lead down to a grand English rose garden, with multiple benches littered throughout with mini firepits near each. Twinkle lights strung back and forth throughout, attached to four lamp post surrounding the garden. Perfect for these chilly early spring evenings. Just beyond the rose garden is a good-size grass lawn with a pathway leading to a gorgeous white gazebo, also strung with twinkle lights.

There are a few things I would change, update, redecorate, and paint inside the house, but I would not touch this backyard. This is something out of a dream. I could spend every evening in this gorgeous garden and never get sick of it.

After we spend some more time looking at every nook and cranny, we decide to go grab a bite at a local spot. We head over to a cute little spot called The Kitchen, and I order the Buddha bowl. Yum!

"I really loved that backyard, but the kitchen at the Ithaca spot was huge!" Alan exclaims.

"Yeah, but do we really need that much of a kitchen?" I ask.

"I am very fond of both properties. It's going to have to come down to you two to make the final choice," Doug says as he tears into his chicken salad sandwich.

"I like things about both too. I can see either one doing really well. It's your choice, Kate," Alan says as they both look at me waiting my answer.

I sit there under there, stares for a minute just staring blankly before I compose myself and answer, "I think it's time for a pros-and-cons list. It's the only way I can make a decision like this," I state calmly while I have a slight panic attack on the inside.

This feels like a huge decision, and I feel all the pressure to make the right business decision, knowing it will affect multiple people's future and lively hoods. We agree to meet back for dinner before heading back to the airport. I need some time to think and compile my list.

* * * * *

The Decision

I chose Alexandria Bay! I bet you didn't see that coming. I couldn't get that amazing rose garden out of mind, the history of the house—everything was like a dream. We got back from New York a few days ago, and we submitted our offer this morning and it got accepted right away. This whole process feels a bit daunting but with Donald assisting and an investor and partner, I feel confident we can pull this off.

Escrow closes in sixty days, and we will be that much closer to opening our new inn in New York. I've got my plate full, calling handymen to come and help with some repairs and updates I want to get done before we open. First, I want to tackle Alan and mine's living quarters. I'm so inspired by the rose garden I'm using as inspiration. The fact that our little house opens right up to outside of the little garden is perfect. Truth be told, I think that was the ultimate selling point for me. Originally, I had not wanted to live at the inn, but having this little private house on the property was perfect and helps keep cost down since I'll be living where I work.

Somehow amid all this planning, I also have to pack up our whole lives and get ready to move across the country. Not to mention all this coincides with Jessica's graduation day. She's going to come with us after graduation and stay in one of the bedrooms in the inn until she leaves in the fall for school and help us get the inn up and running. I'm hoping everything goes according to plan to open by December.

Simone is lining up flights for her and Roxy to come out once Alan, Jessica, and I get there. I'm so relieved they both agreed to come and be a part of this crazy adventure. It's so hard to leave community. I think of all my friends I'm leaving behind in California and how much I will miss them. I know I'll be back, but it's not the same as living in a place. They've been my community for so long, and I just want to pack everyone I love in a carry-on and bring them with me. I know it's unrealistic but let a girl dream. I always say, "If something is hard, then it's usually worth it." It's my little pep talk I give myself to try and get through these hard things. But it really is true. I've done a lot of really hard things in my life, and it's always been worth it. I may have scraped through with battle scars, but like my counselor had said, "There is always a gift."

Now to get through finishing the repairs on Still Waters Inn, Jessica's prom/graduation, packing and planning. Let's go!

6

Jessica Takes Over

Written from Jessica's point of view

Finals are over. *Whew!* With Mom and Dad going back and forth for the new inn, it's been nuts around here. I haven't even told them about the drama with prom. It's a week away, and I still haven't decided what to do. I got asked by two guys, which, in itself, is bonkers. I had just about decided to not go and accept my fate as a forever single-cat lady. I don't have any cats yet, but I'm still young.

Peter asked me before first period, and I told him I'd think about it. He's been such a good friend to me. We have the same taste in movies, and he loves coffee almost as much as me. He's also really funny and gets my strange sense of humor. But then at lunch, Miles asked me. Miles is my comic-book buddy. We always go on comic book runs together and loan each other whatever latest issue we just finished that the other person just has to read. I enjoy his friendship, but I'm not sure we have anything to talk about past comic books, which I wouldn't necessarily hate. And like, am I even over Nick enough to agree to go to prom with someone else? I mean, I guess it's just a night… I'm not committing to marrying them or anything. *Ugh!* Why is being a teenager so hard? Maybe I should make a pros-and-cons list like Mom…nah.

"Ah, saved by the bell!" I say to myself as I answer the door and let my best friend, Rory, in.

"Rory! Help! How do I decide?" I ask in a panic.

"Whoa, whoa, whoa! I thought we were going dress shopping, not dissecting your love life!" exclaims Rory. "I thought you were going with Peter?"

"I thought I was going to say yes too until Miles asked. I don't want to hurt his feelings. He's one of the few people who understand my comic-book obsession," I explain.

"Well, which one are you attracted to?" Rory asks plainly.

Sheepishly, I answer, "Well… Peter. But isn't that superficial to choose based on looks?"

"I don't think it's totally superficial, it's chemistry. You have really great chemistry with Peter, and let's face it, you, guys, have had a crush on each other for a while. This could turn into something with Peter, something more than just a prom date," Rory reasons.

"I think that's what I'm afraid of Rory. I'm not sure I'm ready to get serious with someone new. Am I over Nick enough? What happens when we graduate and leave for college? I'm going to Cal Poly, and he's still undecided. Would I be setting myself up for more heartache? I honestly don't think I can take anymore right now," I explain.

"Jessica, can I be real with you?" Rory asks.

"Of course, you know I value honesty."

"Well, it sounds like your letting fear influence your decision. Is that what you want? You are not usually one who let's fear dictate your life," Rory states.

"No, you're right, Rory. I am afraid. I thought Nick and I were forever. We made promises to each other, we talked about forever, and it was all a lie."

"I know, and it was a really painful thing for you to go through, but you know what will help you heal fully? Going out and having fun, allowing your heart to grow in affection to someone else. Otherwise, you're just going to be stuck forever. It's time to choose. You know my vote is Peter. Miles is a good friend, but that's all he is, and I think it would be cruel to let him think he has a shot at something more."

"Did anyone tell you you're really wise for a seventeen-year-old?" I say to Rory. "You're right, I'll call Peter now, and then we can go dress shopping."

"What about Miles? You need to let him know as well. That one is simple. You just tell him your flattered he asked, but Peter asked first, and you are going with him."

I groan loudly before dialing Peter up.

"Hi, Peter, just calling to say yes, I would like to go to prom with you."

"That's great, Jessica. I'll buy our tickets tomorrow. What color is your dress?" Peter asks.

"Uh, not sure. Rory and I are actually going to go look for dresses now. Wanna grab some pizza at the mall after? Say seven?"

"Sounds great! See you then."

"Oh my gosh! Not only did I say yes to going to prom, but I also asked him to meet us for pizza tonight! Who am I? Did I just ask him on a date?" I am now in full blown panic.

"No, I don't think so. You, guys, have eaten together before, so this isn't new. The only thing that's new is now you are going to prom together. Now let's get to the mall before you change your mind. We've got four hours to try on dresses before we see Peter. I'll call Dean to meet us there for pizza too, so I'm not a third wheel," Rory says as she rushes me out the door and into her car. "And you can call Miles from the car and break the news to him."

I groan as I buckle my seatbelt. When did my life become about making uncomfortable moves?

* * * * *

Prom

What a whirlwind of a week, I think to myself as I smooth my champagne pink silk slip dress. Of course, I paired it with my black combat boots and my black leather jacket. Peter is holding my hand as we enter the gym that's so badly decorated in crepe paper and way too many balloons. I can't say much since I wasn't part of the prom committee. Between finals, my parents' new inn, and my last school play and graduation looming, there was no way I was adding prom decor to my plate.

Peter looks so cute in his black tux and his boyish brown hair falling across his forehead. I can no longer deny that I definitely have feelings for him. Of course, I've had a crush on him for a while. I just thought nothing would ever come of it. High school is almost over, and who knows where life is going to take us.

Okay, I need to stop. Jessica, just enjoy tonight. Stop over-thinking everything. Live in the moment.

"Want to dance?" Peter asks.

"Sure," I reply.

"Cool." He puts his hands around my waist and pulls me close. Of course, it's a slow song, and the butterflies in my stomach really want me to puke, I think.

"Are you ready for opening night?" he asks about the school play.

"Yeah, I think so. How about you?" I ask.

"I'm not sure I have all my lines totally memorized, but I'm close. Maybe we can run lines together later?" replies Peter.

"Sure, I'd like that. I've had so much on my mind with graduation looming, college, family stuff it's been kind of difficult to get into this one."

"Totally understand, you know… I got into Julliard," he says as he looks at my face to see my reaction.

"That's great! Congratulations, that's huge!" I croak out, feeling like I just got punched in the gut.

"I know I've said it before, but I really think you should apply. It's not too late, and the deadline is the day of our last show. I know your dream is to be an actress. This would be a great move for you. People who graduate from Julliard are given so many more opportunities. Plus, I would be there. I don't know if you know this yet, but, Jessica, I really like you. We have grown our friendship the last four years, and I know you had your heart broken with Nick, but I would really love a chance to see if we can grow what we have. You can't deny our chemistry," Peter confesses.

I just blink, unable to form any words, trying to process everything Peter just told me as he holds me, and we glide across the floor of the school gymnasium.

"Jessica?" Peter implores.

"I'm in," I reply. Here goes nothing. Life is all about risk.

Back to Kate in New York

Today is the day to go exploring Alexandria Bay, home of our new inn and our new home. I'm excited and nervous, everything needs to line up, and I still don't have a name for the inn. Still Waters was easy to name. I knew I wanted a place that would house peace. Creating a peaceful atmosphere for guest to come and saturate in has always been a huge piece of the puzzle that is this dream of being an innkeeper. Peace is a nonnegotiable for me.

Peace is the goal always. Grief has reared its head again, despite the excitement that comes with this next chapter in my life. People commonly associate grief with death, which I've experienced my share. But there are many types of loss experiences, including moving. I would say even more so for moving across the country. Grief is defined as the conflicting feelings caused by change of, or the end in, a familiar pattern or behavior. Almost everything you're familiar with changes when you move. A move like we have made can be exciting and scary, but we embrace the new opportunity, while simultaneously being terrified to leave our friends and familiarity we've known for years.

Grief is the normal and natural reaction to loss, yet almost everything we learned about grief is not normal, not natural, and not healthy. You can't say hello to the new until you first say goodbye to the old. During moments of sadness, I think about how comfortable and safe our life has felt these past years, and I think about how scary this new adventure is and how I feel so unsure, and then I close my eyes and refocus on God. He has a peace that surpasses all understanding, I want that. And because He is a good Father, we have access to that peace through Jesus Christ.

> Do not be anxious about anything, but in every situation, by prayer and petition, with thanksgiving, present your request to God. And the peace of God, which transcends all understanding, will guard your hearts and your minds in Christ Jesus. (Philippians 4:6–7)

> In peace I will both lie down and sleep; for you alone, O Lord, make me dwell in safety. (Psalm 4:8)

We just flew in last night after Jessica's final performance of high school plays. It's hard to believe my baby is almost done with high school. One more month. Alan stayed behind this time to tie up some lose ends, then after Jessica graduates, we will all move up here. Jessica will help out until college in the fall, and then if all goes as planned, we will open up in November. Just in time for holiday travelers.

Thankfully the floors have been replaced, and the pipes are in perfect working order as is Still Waters Inn. It's hard to imagine that it's running perfectly without me; it almost feels like I'm letting go of another child. For so long I was a 100 percent hands on, steering the ship, and now it's going on without me. Swimmingly, I might add. A mixture of feelings rush through, a touch of grief, a dash of excitement, and a blanket of peace envelope my heart.

Going through the clothes I packed, I carefully select my best "adventuring" outfit. My olive-green linen pants, my combat boots with a sweet floral print covering the white leather, and my white Schitt's Creek T-shirt. (Ew, David, don't judge me. We all have our guilty pleasures.) I tie my long red hair in two braids and throw a bandana in there for good measure. Cute, comfortable, and versatile, if I don't say so myself. I grab my bag and head out to meet the crew.

Donald, Simone, Roxy, and I stroll down the road to the nearest diner to grab breakfast. We see a little place that's open for breakfast called Riley's by the River.

"This looks promising," Roxy remarks.

"If they have eggs and bacon, I will be a happy camper," declares Donald.

Grabbing a booth near the entrance, we are greeted as soon as we sit down by our waitress. "Good morning gang, I'm Priscilla. Can I grab you some coffees?"

We all respond with a resounding yes and open our menus as Priscilla heads off to grab us some much-needed caffeination.

By the time Priscilla returns with steaming hot mugs of liquid gold, we are ready to order breakfast.

"What'll it be gang?" Priscilla asks as she licks the tip of her pencil ready to jot down our breakfast order.

"I'll have the Frittata," Simone responds.

"I'll try the crab cake benedicts. That sounds delish," Roxy orders.

"You had me at breakfast buffet," states Donald.

"And I'll have 'That's My Jam Omelet,'" I add.

As Priscilla heads off to give our orders to the cooks, an older man at the booth next to ours turns around.

"You all visiting our great Alexandria Bay?" he asks.

"As a matter of fact, we just bought the old inn down the street. I'm Kate, this is Simone, Roxy, and Donald."

"Well, I'll be, wasn't sure anyone would ever buy that old place. My name is Harvard, but everyone around these parts just calls me ol' man Harley. Feel free to do likewise."

"Great to meet you, Harley. Would you care to pull up a chair and join us? I'd love to hear about Alexandria Bay from a long time local such as yourself," I ask.

"Sure! I love telling stories to anyone who would like to hear them," replies Harley.

"Well, we are here and are ready to hear."

Unanimous groans come from Simone and Roxy, "It's too early for wordplay, Kate."

Harley pulls up a chair and brings his plate of pancakes and mug of coffee over and gets settled down just as Priscilla arrives with our breakfast.

"You wouldn't be bugging these poor tourists now would you, ol' man Harley?" Priscilla asks suspiciously.

"Not at all," Donald interjects, "he's graciously volunteered to teach us about the village."

"All right then, enjoy your breakfast and let me know if you need anything else. I'll be back soon to warm up your coffees," Priscilla says as she walks away to check on her next table.

"So, Harley, give us the scoop," I say as we all look with expectancy to hear from this sweet old man in front of us.

"Well, Alexandria Bay is the heart of the Thousand Islands. Long before Europeans settled here, Iroquois and Algonquin spent their summer months here, fishing and hunting on the river.

"Lore has it that Manitou, the peoples' great spirit, said to his people, 'I will give you a paradise if you live in peace.' According to legend, the tribes did not stop fighting, so the great spirit put his paradise, known as Manitouana, the Garden of the Great Spirit, into a great blanket to take back into the sky. Just as he was to part the sky curtain, the blanket fell open and the garden splashed into the St. Lawrence River. As it struck the water, it broke into hundreds upon hundreds of pieces, big and little, creating the Thousand Islands," Harley explains.

"Wow! That's fascinating," I reply.

"How about the Boldt Castle? It's so beautiful, I can't wait to go tour it!" Roxy asks excitedly.

"Oh sure!" replies Harley. "The Boldt Castle stands today as a tribute to the love story of a Mr. George C. Boldt and his wife Louise. George had one of America's greatest rags-to-riches stories. They say he was only thirteen when he immigrated to America from the small Prussian Isle of Rügen. George started at the bottom, working in hotel kitchens throughout New York City. Young George had ambition and a gift for diplomacy. He became the millionaire proprietor of New York City's Waldorf-Astoria and the owner of Bellevue-Stratford Hotel in Philadelphia."

"That's so cool! I've been to the Waldorf-Astoria, and it's breathtaking. It's wild to think it's been around for so long. Such a rich history," I interject.

"Well, in the 1890s, George and his wife Louise began vacationing in the Thousand Islands. Eventually George purchased the now famous Heart Island, a property he planned to transform into the ultimate gift of love for his darling wife. In 1900, George hired the most skilled masons and architect's money could buy to create his own version of a Rhineland Castle. Construction on Boldt Castle was well underway when tragedy struck. In January 1904, George sent all his workers a telegram saying, 'Stop all work. Louise has died.' Heartbroken, George never returned to Heart Island again." Harley pauses for dramatic effect as we all wipe the moisture from our eyes.

"The Boldt castle was abandoned to the elements and vandals for seventy-three years." Harley continues. "It was not until 1977 that the Thousand Islands Bridge authority was gifted the historic Boldt property. Since then, the TI Bridge has transformed the ruins of Boldt Castle into a premier attraction for the one thousand islands. The evolving Boldt Castle is an absolute must see and has thousands of annual visitors!

"Okay, ol' man Harley, why do you sound like a travel brochure?" Donald asks suspiciously.

"You got me. I'm a tour guide by trade during the tourist season, May through October," replies Harley sheepishly.

"Hey!" I interject, "That's perfect! We planned on exploring the Island today. Could we hire you to be our tour guide? You obviously are super knowledgeable, I'd love to pick your brain. This could really help us give our guests at the inn the optimal stay while they are here."

"Well, an adventure with you lot sounds like an okay time to me!" states Harley.

"Great!" I exclaim as I pull out my day planner. "Where do you suggest we start? I'm very interested in everything the village and islands have to offer, but it is a bit daunting finding a jumping off point.

"Seems like we should grab some bikes and do a village tour, that way we can burn off our breakfast. It's how I keep my girlish figure, and then head toward the marina so we can catch a ferry to Heart Island and have lunch at Boldt Castle. If you don't already have a sandwich packed up, you better go ahead and flag Priscilla down and have her wrap something up for you. There is a great little spot on the grounds with a picnic table under a great big pine tree. Perfect little eatin' spot."

I jotted down our plan for our day as tourist as we all finished our breakfast. I can't believe how everything has come together so perfectly! Meeting Harley is truly a godsent miracle. He is so knowledgeable, and aside from our tour today, I foresee a very long and prosperous friendship with ol' man Harley. Maybe I can convince him to make himself available for our guest. I'm making a note to discuss later with Donald how we can get Harley on our payroll. Can you imagine having a bona fide, very experienced tour guide on staff at the inn who can answer every question they didn't even know they had? Unreal. I've still got to come up with a name for this inn. I'm really hoping that today will inspire me, and I will go to sleep tonight having a name for our brand-new inn in Alexandria Bay. I keep thinking about the story Harley told us about the great spirit and his paradise blanket. Hmmm… Paradise Blanket Inn? Definitely not. Keep thinking, Kate.

As we finish our meals and decide where to rent our tour bikes for the morning, our waitress Priscilla comes back to check on us.

"Are we all finished here, gang?" she asks. "Anymore coffee refills? Breakfast dessert? Hey, don't knock it until you've tried it."

"Breakfast dessert? Very tempting, but I'm stuffed," states Donald. We all echo his response.

"Priscilla, we would actually love to order some lunch items to go. Would you be able to wrap our orders up? We are doing a bike tour of the village and then will make our way to Boldt Castle where Harley says there is a must eat at picnic bench." I laugh.

"Sure thing! People do it all the time, and we are happy to oblige. What'll you have?" Priscilla grabs out her notepad and pencil to jot down our lunch orders.

"I'll have a turkey club," orders Roxy.

"I'll do a cobb salad. Can you throw in a fork and some napkins," asks Simone.

"No problem," replies Priscilla. "Next?"

"I'll take a Reuben please," orders Donald.

"And I'll try Sam's chicken salad with no bleu cheese please," I add.

"All right, I got one turkey club, one cobb, one Reuben, and one Sam's chicken salad, no bleu cheese. How about you, Harley? Would you like your usual?" Priscilla asks.

"You know me too well, Priscilla dear. I will take my usual double wrapped please," Harley responds.

"Sit tight, gang, I'll bring out your checks, and your food will be up soon." Priscilla takes off to gives our orders to the kitchen.

"I have a new goal, guys," I state. "I want to eventually try everything on this menu. It looks so good! Hopefully I can meet that goal without gaining five hundred pounds."

"That's a mighty fine goal there, missy," interjects Harley. "But I wouldn't worry none much about your figure. Looks mighty fine to me if you don't mind me saying so, and you'll be walking or bike riding so much, none of your food will have time to stick to you."

"You're so kind, Harley." I blush.

"Good thing Alan isn't here. He might give you the stink eye," says Donald.

"Oh, I don't mean any harm. I just get so sad when people can't see themselves how they really are. I believe it's our job to help people see what God sees in them, pull the gold out of them with our words and actions. It's one of the best parts of my job because I get to meet so many different people with all sorts of different backgrounds. Besides visiting Alexandria Bay, the one thing they all have in common is their need for kindness. For someone to see them the way the good Lord sees them and try and help them see it too."

"Harley, I think you just became my new best friend," I say swiping an errant tear from my eye.

"Hey!" exclaim Roxy and Simone in unison.

"Roxy, Simone, you know you both are irreplaceable," I say with a chuckle.

Priscilla returns with our checks, and Donald reaches for Harley's bill and looks him in the eyes, "Please let me take care of your meals today. It's the least I can do."

"Well, that's mighty kind of you. I have a feeling Old Alexandria Bay is in for quite a treat having you all join us here. You are just the kind of folks we need here," Harley adds.

8

After an amazing time exploring Alexandria Bay, we've come back to Cali for Jessica's graduation before officially move to the East Coast. I have so many emotions between losing my one and only baby girl to the throws of adulthood to leaving my dream home, family, and community that I've built history with to embark on the great unknown. I was listening to this song this morning, and the words really hit me. Honestly, I cried because I related so deeply with what the singers were conveying.

> *What a friend we have in Jesus, all our sins and*
> *griefs to bear*
> *What a privilege it is to carry everything to God*
> *in prayer.*
> *Some things we have not, because we ask not.*
> *When we have a friend who's there, He's there.*
> *When we're weak and heavy laden, encumbered*
> *with a load of care.*
> *We should never be discouraged when we*
> *Take it to the Lord in prayer.*
> *Oh what peace we often forfeit*
> *Oh what needless pain we bear*
> *We should never be discouraged when we*
> *Take it to the Lord in prayer.*

I know the goodness of God, I've tasted, and I've seen. Yet my flesh is weak, and I despair. It's human to fear in the face of the unknown—to step out in faith in one of the biggest risks I've ever taken in my life—but I must repeat my personal mantra. Well, two of them actually. Hard things are usually worth it, and why would I not be willing to have heartache when my best friend is the Healer (Jesus).

Now that, Jessica is officially a high school graduate, and all our personal items are either sold off or have been picked up by movers it's time to celebrate. Our last party at Still Waters Inn for the foreseeable future is Jessica's graduation party. All her friends and our community have rallied together to celebrate her and say goodbye to the Brown's or at least "see ya later."

I should maybe be concerned about her new romance with her longtime friend Peter, but oddly I'm not. He treats her good, and she seems genuinely happy, so I can't complain. Of course, I worry about her heart and well-being. I always will. She's my baby, college student or not.

It's not the season for them, but she requested I make my pumpkin butterscotch cookies since she won't get them this fall. Of course, you and I both know I will be sending my baby regular care packages with homemade cookies. In addition to the cookies, we had pizza and dinosaur-shaped chicken nuggets—some of her favorite foods. I chuckle to myself. This young woman still has so many sweet innocent attributes that I cherish. Her childlikeness is a rare and beautiful thing in a culture that hardens you and forces so many to grow up much faster than they should. She has been blessed with a beautiful mixture of wisdom and innocence. Reminds me of the scripture Matthew 10:16b: "Be as wise as serpents and gentle as doves."

"Hey, Mom, Dad, I have something to tell you," Jessica says as she pulls Alan and myself aside.

"What is it?" I ask, immediately thinking the worse.

"I got into Julliard. I'm moving to NYC!" Jessica exclaims.

"What happen to Cal Poly? I thought you wanted to be by the beach. You've been talking about it forever," Alan asks.

"I know, but you, guys, will be in New York, and Peter is going to Julliard and encouraged me to apply. There are so many more opportunities for actors in New York. Plus, I'll be close by you guys!" she explains.

"Well, I don't hate that," I say as I give her a big hug.

"Mom, no hugs!" Jessica resists.

"Sorry, I'm your mother. I have hug privileges that cannot be revoked." I laugh.

"Dad too!" Alan says as he pulls us both into his big arms for a big family embrace.

This moment, whatever else happens or doesn't happen, I am so grateful to God for my family. They are the ultimate gift that I did nothing to deserve, yet because of His grace and mercy and because He is a good, good Father who gives good gifts, I have two of the greatest gifts I will ever have in life, Alan and Jessica.

A man's heart plans his way, But the Lord directs his steps. (Proverbs 16:9)

The End

Recipe for pumpkin butterscotch cookies

- 2 1/4 cups all-purpose flour
- 1 tsp baking soda
- 1/2 tsp salt
- 2 tsp pumpkin spice seasoning
- 1 cup (2 sticks) butter, softened
- 3/4 cup brown sugar
- 3/4 cup granulated sugar
- 2 large eggs
- 1 tsp vanilla extract
- 1/3 cup pumpkin puree
- 1 2/3 cups butterscotch chips

Instructions

1. Preheat oven 350
2. In small bowl combine flour, baking soda, salt, and pumpkin spice
3. In a large mixing bowl, beat butter, granulated sugar, brown sugar, eggs, and vanilla
4. Beat in flour mixture gradually
5. Add in pumpkin puree, mix thoroughly
6. Stir in butterscotch chips
7. Drop onto ungreased baking sheets by rounded tablespoon
8. Bake for 9 minutes. Cool on baking sheet for 2 minutes. Transfer to wire racks to cool completely.

Enjoy!
Notes: Add dark chocolate chips or dried cranberries with butterscotch chips for an added fun flavor!

About the Author

Kathy Branning was born and raised in Southern California. Kathy and her family have recently planted roots in New York City's beautiful Financial District.

Kathy uses her writing to process grief, experience, and share healing with her readers. She hopes you are inspired and uplifted as you follow her characters on their journey through family reconciliation, grief, self-exploration, friendship, faith, hope, and love.

Kathy considers her faith and family to be most important to her. If she isn't spending time with her friends and family, you can almost always find her around her sweet bichon Maltese mix, Snow White.

It's an Inn-Side Job is a tale of an innkeeper, which is the second book in the *Tales of an Innkeeper* series and sequel to *'Tis So Suite: Tales of an Innkeeper*, Kathy's first published book.

www.ingramcontent.com/pod-product-compliance
Lightning Source LLC
Chambersburg PA
CBHW022115150726
47990CB00003B/1353